Copyright © 2001 by Nord-Süd Verlag AG, Gossau Zürich, Switzerland
First published in Switzerland under the title *Ich wars nicht!*
English translation copyright © 2001 by North-South Books Inc.

First published in the United States, Great Britain, Canada,
Australia, and New Zealand in 2001 by North-South Books,
an imprint of Nord-Süd Verlag AG, Gossau Zürich, Switzerland.

Distributed in the United States by North-South Books Inc., New York.

Library of Congress Cataloging-in-Publication Data is available.
A CIP catalogue record for this book is available from The British Library.

ISBN 0-7358-1523-2 (TRADE BINDING)
1 3 5 7 9 TB 10 8 6 4 2
ISBN 0-7358-1524-0 (LIBRARY BINDING)
1 3 5 7 9 LB 10 8 6 4 2
Printed in Germany

For more information about our books, and the authors and artists
who create them, visit our web site: www.northsouth.com

Udo Weigelt

It Wasn't Me!

Illustrated by Julia Gukova

Translated by J. Alison James

North-South Books

NEW YORK · LONDON

One fine day, Ferret found a bush covered with ripe raspberries. Delighted, he started to pick them. Back and forth he ran, until he had a huge pile of raspberries. But when he returned from picking the fruit on the other side of the bush, his entire pile of berries had disappeared.

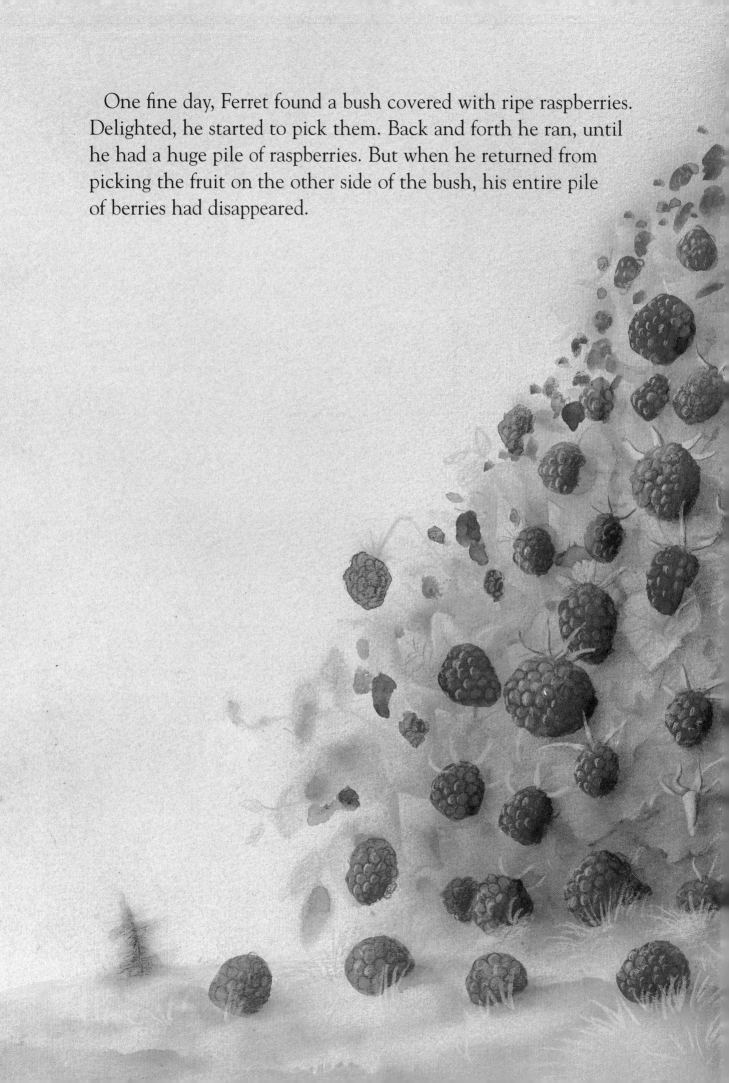

Where could they have gone? Ferret searched all around, but there was no trace left of all his beautiful berries.

Mouse came along, and Ferret told her everything.

"They just disappeared?" asked Mouse, amazed.

"Just like that!" cried Ferret. "I turned my back for a moment and suddenly they were gone. All my hard work was for nothing."

"They must have been stolen," Mouse said. "And if they were stolen, I have a good idea who could have done it."

Mouse ran off, and Ferret followed.

They came to a tree. High in the branches perched Raven.
"Hey up there!" cried Mouse. "Did you steal Ferret's raspberries?"
"Me? Of course not!" said Raven. "Why did you come straight to me?"
"Because you stole something before," said Mouse, and that was true.
"But I don't steal anymore!" cried Raven. "And I didn't take the raspberries either."

"Then what is this?" cried Mouse suddenly. She plucked a raspberry from right under Raven's tree and held it high.

"I don't know anything about that," said Raven, baffled. "It doesn't belong to me."

"That's right," said Ferret. "That raspberry belongs to me. So you did steal again! And you dropped one of my raspberries here on the ground."

"But that isn't true, not true at all!" cried Raven in despair.

"You are a thief!" accused Mouse. "A thief and a liar, because you won't confess to what you've done."

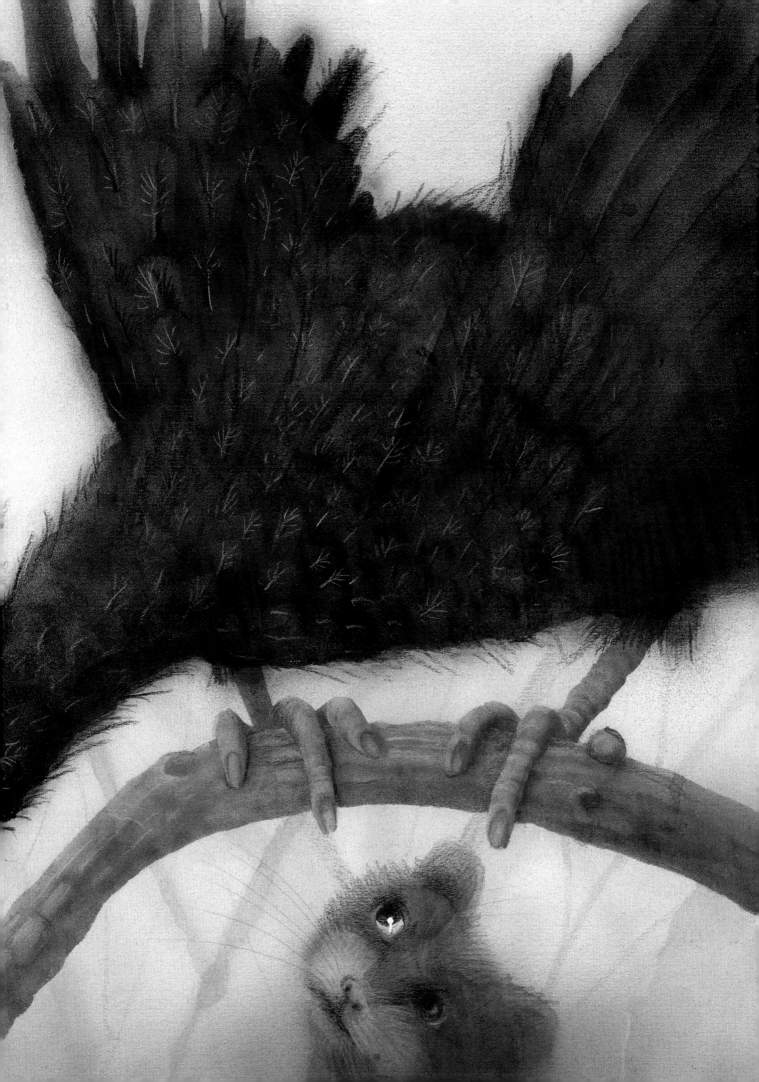

Mouse and Ferret left Raven. They called a meeting of the animals. Everyone should hear what had happened and decide what to do about Raven.

Mouse told the whole story. The animals were very indignant.

"It's odd, though," said Hamster, "that Raven keeps saying she didn't do it. Last time she stole something, at least she confessed."

"That's true," said Hedgehog. "But Mouse did find the raspberry right underneath Raven's tree."

Everybody agreed that the raspberry was a real clue. At last they decided that Raven must have stolen again.

When Raven finally came to the animal meeting, all the others were angry with her.

"Stealing once we can forgive," Hamster said, "but doing it again, we can't tolerate."

Raven didn't know what to say at first. But then she grew angry. "It wasn't me!" she cried. "And if you don't believe me, I'll go and live in a different forest where the animals are kind and trust me."

Then she flew away.

The animals were shocked. They ran after Raven.

"Do you promise it wasn't you?" asked Hedgehog.

"I swear," Raven said quickly.

So all the animals began to search more carefully for clues. After a while, Hamster found another raspberry, not too far from Raven's tree. And then they found another. Nervously they followed the trail. Who had stolen the raspberries? Could he be dangerous?

Then suddenly they saw the most amazing sight. A long row of raspberries was moving through the grass.

"But that can't be!" cried Hamster. "Raspberries can't walk!"

Carefully they tiptoed after the berries, which were snaking around a little hill and then vanishing.

All the animals watched as the last raspberry disappeared—down into an anthill!

"Ants!" cried Hedgehog. "The ants have taken the raspberries, not Raven! They dropped one under her tree. That's why we thought that she had stolen the berries."

The guard ants had climbed up to the top of the anthill to look at the intruders.

"We'll get the raspberries back," Raven said determinedly.

"But how?" whispered Hedgehog. "We can't dig them out. The anthill is much too deep."

"And ants bite," Hamster said, and shivered.

But Raven was determined.

"We'd like to speak with your Queen," she said to the guard ants. "We want the raspberries back!"

"No way," said one of the ants. "Finders keepers. And that's final."

"All right," said Raven sweetly. "Ants taste almost as good as raspberries."

"Ants? Taste good? Just a minute," cried the ant and he disappeared into the anthill.

In a moment, the Ant Queen appeared before them.

"Your majesty, your ants have stolen Ferret's raspberries! We ask that you give them back immediately," Hamster said.

"Stolen? Ridiculous," said the Ant Queen. "Our job is to keep the woods neat and tidy. That is what we do. When something is lying around, we pick it up and bring it home. The raspberries were just lying there, so of course we brought them home."

"But they were Ferret's berries," said Hedgehog. "They didn't belong to you."

The Ant Queen thought about this. "Well," she said at last, "just this once we will return the raspberries. But if you leave something lying around again that tastes good, you'd better watch out!"

The Queen told the ants to bring the berries up. Soon there was a huge pile of ripe raspberries, and all the animals should have been happy. But they still felt terrible about accusing Raven.

"I am truly sorry that I didn't believe you," apologized Mouse.
Ferret was so ashamed that he told Raven she could have all
the raspberries.

Raven was the only one who was happy. She was so happy that
she decided right then and there to have a Great Raspberry Feast.
"And I invite all of you," she said gleefully. "Even the ants!"

So Ferret, Mouse, Hamster, Hedgehog, Raven, and thousands of
ants ate sweet red raspberries until they couldn't eat another bite.